Meg, Mu...
and the Donkey

Written by Simon Puttock
Illustrated by Sabine Cazassus

Collins

Meg and Mum took their donkey to market.

Mum said, "Up you go!"

Oof!

3

So Mum rode.

Oof!

5

So Mum and Meg both rode.

Oof!

So Mum and Meg carried the donkey.

9

Soon Mum and Meg needed a rest ...

And the donkey got away!

A donkey's day

Ideas for reading

Written by Clare Dowdall, PhD
Lecturer and Primary Literacy Consultant

Reading objectives:

- use phonic knowledge to decode regular words and read them aloud accurately
- read and understand simple sentences
- demonstrate understanding when talking with others about what they have read

Communication and language objectives:

- develop their own narratives and explanations by connecting ideas or events
- follow instructions involving several ideas or actions

Curriculum links: Personal, Social and Emotional Development

Resources: pencils, paper, sticky notes

High frequency words: to, the, mum

Interest words: donkey, market, lazy, girl, cruel, poor, carried

Word count: 60

Build a context for reading

- Ask children to share what they know about donkeys, using questions to stimulate the discussion, e.g. *What type of creature is a donkey? Who has ridden on a donkey? What are donkeys used for?*
- Ask children to look at the donkey on the front cover and suggest what they think his character is like.
- Read the title and blurb to the children. Ask children to suggest who will ride the donkey and why.

Understand and apply reading strategies

- Turn to pp2–3. Read the text to the children. Model how to respond to speech marks and exclamation marks by reading with an expressive voice.
- Look at the words *donkey* and *market*. Remind children of the strategies that they can use to read longer words, e.g. sounding out and blending, looking for familiar chunks (*don-key, mark-et*), using the context, checking whether the word makes sense in the sentence.
- Look at the speech bubble. Ask children to suggest what the donkey is thinking when he says, "Oof!"